Produced by Kroha Associates, Inc.
Middletown, Connecticut.

Printed in the United States of America.

ISBN 1-56326-104-9

I Miss You, Daisy

By Ruth Lerner Perle

One bright morning Minnie Mouse was on her way to school. As usual, she stopped to pick up Daisy on her way. But before Minnie had a chance to ring the bell, Daisy came running out to meet her, shouting, "Guess what! Guess what, Minnie! I'm going to sleep-away camp as soon as school is over."

"But, but..." Minnie stammered. "School will be over in just a few days!"

"That's right!" Daisy shouted. "I can hardly wait."

Minnie had a funny feeling in her stomach. "Does that mean you'll be gone all summer, and we won't see each other?"

"I'll only be gone for a month," Daisy said.

The next day, Minnie watched Daisy pack her camp suitcases. She helped her pick out shorts and T-shirts and sweaters. Daisy talked about all the things she would be doing at camp — swimming, boating, volleyball, arts and crafts, and even horseback riding.

Minnie tried to be cheerful, but in her heart she felt sad.

"I'm glad for you, Daisy," she said. "But I know I'm going to miss you."

The next few days passed quickly. Soon school was over for the summer and it was time for Daisy to leave.

When Daisy came to say good-bye to her friend, Minnie gave her a little package. It was a box full of pretty pink writing paper, envelopes, and postcards.

"That's to make sure you write to me," Minnie said, wiping a tear from her eye.

"Oh, Minnie!" Daisy said. "Of course I'll write! I'll write just as often as I can, I promise."

"So will I," said Minnie. "You can count on it."

The two girls walked to the place where the camp bus was to pick up Daisy.

When the bus came, Daisy said good-bye and climbed in.

Minnie stood waving until the bus disappeared around the corner.

Minnie ran home and looked at her calendar. She took a blue crayon and marked all the days that Daisy would be gone. Then, with a red crayon, she drew a circle around the day Daisy would come back. She counted the days.

"How will I be able to wait so long?" she wondered.

With Daisy away, nothing seemed quite as much fun as it usually did.

One day, Minnie played dress up with Clarabelle and Lilly. She had a good time, but it wasn't as much fun as when Daisy was there.

On another day, Minnie went for pizza with Penny, but it didn't taste as good as when she shared a slice with Daisy.

At home, Minnie tried to read her books, but nothing seemed interesting, and she couldn't concentrate.

Even her favorite TV programs all seemed boring.

Fifi jumped into her lap, as if to say, *You have me!* but it didn't seem to help. Minnie just kept thinking of Daisy, wondering what she was doing and when she would write. It seemed as though the summer would never end.

Every morning Minnie ran out to the mailbox to see if there was a letter from Daisy, but the mailbox was always empty.

Minnie was feeling lonelier and lonelier as each day passed. And the lonelier she felt, the angrier she got.

Then, one day, when Minnie went out to look in her mailbox, it was stuffed full of mail. There were eight letters, six postcards, and a little package. They were all from Daisy!

"I guess the mail must have been held up," the mailman said. "I see that some of these letters were sent some time ago."

"Thank you, thank you!" Minnie shouted, and she ran inside to read her mail.

Daisy's letters were full of news. She told about her counselor (yay!), about the food (boo!), and about Lisa, a special new friend she'd made. She wrote about all the fun they were having together and about the secrets that they shared.

Minnie opened the package. It was full of camp pictures. Most of them were of Daisy and Lisa together.

After that, Minnie received a letter from Daisy almost every day, and she felt a lot better. But she couldn't help wondering if Daisy would still be her special friend when she returned.

Then one morning Minnie looked at her calendar and cried, "Hooray! Daisy's coming home this afternoon!"

Minnie spent the whole morning getting ready. First she prepared a
batch of Daisy's favorite cookies.

Then she got out all of Daisy's favorite games and tapes. Finally,
Minnie hung a big WELCOME HOME sign on her front door.

When everything was ready, Minnie changed into clean clothes, picked a small bunch of flowers, and ran to wait for the bus that would bring Daisy home.

As she was waiting, Minnie had a funny feeling. *What if Daisy has changed?* she thought. *What if she doesn't like me anymore?*

Suddenly a yellow bus turned the corner and stopped right in front of Minnie. Her heart was pounding. She looked up at the windows to see if she could spot Daisy. And then, all at once, there she was!

Daisy ran into Minnie's open arms. "Minnie! Minnie! Minnie!" she shouted. "I'm so glad to see you again. I had a wonderful time at camp and I met lots of kids, and learned lots of new things, but I never had as much fun as we have when we are together. I was really afraid you would forget me."

"Oh, Daisy, I missed you *so* much," Minnie said. "I'm happy you had a good time, but I'm even happier that you are back home again with me."

Write to me about someone you missed. Please use the enclosed letter.